He forgot to say "**Excuse me**". Giraffe tripped up. But Rhino was in such a hurry that he didn't stop to help him and he didn't say "**sorry**".

On his birthday Rhino was **very excited**. All his friends came to his party. All his friends gave him lots of presents. But Rhino was so excited that he forgot to thank them. Everyone thought he was **ungrateful** not to say **"Thank you"**.

Lunchtimes were worst of all. Rhino was always very hungry for his lunch. Sometimes he **pushed** to the front of the queue.

When Mrs Croc asked him what he wanted
to eat, he just **pointed** and said **"Pie"**.
He completely forgot to say **"Please"**.
Mrs Croc thought he was **very rude**.

Rhino always forgot to eat with his **mouth closed**.

He loved talking to his friends at lunchtime, too, but he forgot to **finish his mouthful** first.

Worst of all, he thought it was a **good joke** to burp loudly at the table. He thought everyone would **laugh** and think he was **funny**.
But no one thought he was funny at all.
They thought he was **rude**.

13

On Monday, Lion invited all his friends to tea on Friday after school. But Lion didn't invite Rhino. Rhino was **upset**. He didn't like being **left out**. Rhino asked Lion why he hadn't been invited to tea.

Lion said that Rhino didn't always have **nice manners**. He said his mum would not like it if Rhino forgot to say "please" and "thank you" or if he burped loudly.

Rhino was sad. He told his friends he was sorry that he was not polite. He said that he wished he remembered to have good manners all the time. He asked his friends to help him.

They said it was important to **practise good manners** every day. They said it was important to **think about others** and to be polite. Rhino said he would try really hard.

The next day, Rhino tried really hard to be polite. When he wanted to get past Hippo in the playground, he didn't push past him. Instead he politely said "**Excuse me**".

Rhino held the door open for Miss Bird.
Miss Bird thanked him. She said he had **very nice manners**. Rhino was pleased.

At lunchtime, Rhino asked Mrs Croc politely for some pie. He remembered to say **"Please"** and **"Thank you"**.

He remembered to eat with his **mouth closed**.
He didn't burp at all... not once! Everyone thought
Rhino was being very polite.

On Friday, Lion had a special surprise for Rhino. He asked him to tea after school with all the others. Rhino was very excited. He promised that he would **remember his manners**.

23

Lion's mum had made a **wonderful tea**.
Although Rhino was hungry,
he remembered to say
"please" and "thank you".

He remembered to eat with
his mouth closed.

… and he didn't talk with his mouth full.
Everyone thought he had **very nice manners**.

Soon it was time to go home. Rhino remembered to thank Lion's mum for having him to tea **without anyone reminding him!**

Rhino told Lion it was **much nicer to be polite** and to have good manners than to be rude.

A note about sharing this book

The *Behaviour Matters* series has been developed to provide a starting point for further discussion on children's behaviour both in relation to themselves and others. The series is set in the jungle with animal characters reflecting typical behaviour traits often seen in young children.

Rhino Learns to be Polite
This story looks at the importance of having good manners and being polite and considerate towards other people.

How to use the book
The book is designed for adults to share with either an individual child, or a group of children, and as a starting point for discussion.

The book also provides visual support and repeated words and phrases to build reading confidence.

Before reading the story
Choose a time to read when you and the children are relaxed and have time to share the story.

Spend time looking at the illustrations and talk about what the book might be about before reading it together.

Encourage children to employ a phonics first approach to tackling new words by sounding the words out.

After reading, talk about the book with the children:

- Talk about the story with the children. Encourage them to retell the events in chronological order.

- Talk about Rhino's behaviour. Do the children think he always meant to be rude? Point out that sometimes he was just too excited to remember his manners, for example on his birthday. Sometimes he thought he was being funny and simply wanted to make others laugh. Ask the children if they have sometimes forgotten their manners when they have been excited. Invite them to share their experiences with the others.

- Ask the children why they think it is important to be polite. If someone is rude to them how do they feel?

- Talk about the good manners expected of them in their own families, for example not interrupting others when they are speaking; remembering to say 'please' and 'thank you'; eating with their mouth closed etc. Make a list of the common rules that most families share.

- Place the children into two groups. Ask each group to make up a short play about being at a friend's birthday party. Ask them to demonstrate the good manners they should use.

- Invite each group to show their play to the others. At the end, discuss the good manners that were highlighted by each group. Did everyone think the same things were important, for example did both groups think it important to say 'please' and 'thank you' during the party? Did both groups remember to thank the host for having them?

29

For Isabelle, William A, William G, George, Max, Emily,
Leo, Caspar, Felix, Tabitha, Phoebe and Harry – S.G.

First published in Great Britain in 2018
by The Watts Publishing Group

Series Editor: Jackie Hamley
Series Designer: Cathryn Gilbert

A CIP catalogue record for this book is
available from the British Library.

HB ISBN 978 1 4451 5869 3
PB ISBN 978 1 4451 5870 9

Printed in China

Franklin Watts
An imprint of
Hachette Children's Group
Part of The Watts Publishing Group
Carmelite House
50 Victoria Embankment
London EC4Y 0DZ

An Hachette UK Company
www.hachette.co.uk

www.franklinwatts.co.uk

FSC
www.fsc.org
MIX
Paper from
responsible sources
FSC® C104740